CHAOS AND COLD FEET

KARI LEE TOWNSEND

OLIVER
HEBER
BOOKS

Published by Oliver-Heber Books

0 9 8 7 6 5 4 3 2 1

To my own husband of 32 years, Brian. I would say I do all over again. You make life fun, and I wouldn't want to go through it with anyone else. Love you lots.

"I'm so excited for today. You and Mitch are going to make the perfect godparents." My best friend, Joanne West, thrust a male version of her Amazon Irish self—red hair and fiery temper to boot—into my wary arms.

"I hope you're right," I said, looking into the most innocent, baby-soft face. "What do you think, Jeremiah? Will I be a good godmother?"

Wide smokey gray eyes stared up at me, giving me hope for about two seconds. His little cherub cheeks scrunched up as he let out a bellowing squall to rival his Sasquatch father. Jo plopped a pacifier in his gaping mouth without missing a beat, and the screaming infant settled. She had only been a mother for a month and was already a natural.

"No worries, doll, you'll get the hang of it." She blew a kiss at me, looking fabulous and glowing with happiness. Meanwhile, the holes in my spikey blond hair still hadn't filled in after Raoulle from Pump Up the Volume salon talked with his hands a little too much the last time I was there.

"If you say so," I mumbled, my arms trembling

with the weight of my new responsibility and the fear that I would be terrible at it.

Her new husband, Cole West, handed baby Collin —a calm, happy replica of himself with dark hair and dark eyes—to my fiancé, Detective Mitch Stone. They were best friends and Cole trusted Mitch with his life, especially after Mitch had saved him when he was framed for murder and had nearly lost everything. "You got this, buddy." He straightened his tie, his neck tattoo peeking above the collar of his shirt. He looked just as tough in a suit with his buzz cut edged sharply and his muscles straining at the seams.

"I'll try my best." Mitch shook his hands out as if shaking off his nerves before gently taking the angelic baby in his muscular arms. He was a big guy, but even Mitch was dwarfed by Cole. Judging by the size of their offspring, the twins were going to be just as big, if not bigger than their parents.

"I hope the rain stops." Jo looked out the stained-glass windows at the downpour happening outside.

"You and me both," I replied. "Our wedding is in a few weeks, and the reception is supposed to be outside in my backyard. At this rate it's going to be a soggy mess rather than an idyllic sanctuary like I want."

"It will be fine," Mitch chimed in, not looking troubled at all. "They say April showers bring May flowers."

"And mud," Cole said, earning him a scowl from his wife. "I mean, you have a tent, so you'll be good," he quickly added.

"I hope so." I took a deep breath and tried to put my fears aside. Mitch and I had been through so much together with ups and downs and murders derailing our relationship along the way. We were finally in a good place. I loved him with all my heart and knew he loved me. I knew for certain I wanted to spend the rest of my life with this man. Even my cat Morty had come around and softened toward my fiancé.

So why did I have this uneasy feeling in the pit of my stomach?

I chalked it up to standing at the altar in a church. I hadn't been to church in quite a while, but I was a confirmed Catholic, which qualified me to be a godmother. Mitch was also Catholic, but he too hadn't been to church in some time. Neither one of us quite understood what Jo and Cole had been thinking when they chose us.

Father Comstock joined us at the altar and welcomed everyone to this blessed event. Jo's cousin Zoe Burnham and her boyfriend Sean O'Malley—who also worked for Jo at Smokey Jo's Tavern—sat in the front wooden pew with Cole's cousin Diana West. Beside them sat Jo's family, and right in the row behind them sat my parents, Vivian and Donald Meadows. The crowd hushed and, for a moment, I felt like we were at our wedding.

The pit in my stomach grew into a tighter knot.

Father's words snapped me out of my daze, reminding me we were at the babies' christening and not our wedding. The relief I felt troubled me. Sensing my unease, Mitch winked at me, and I smiled in thanks, relaxing a little for the first time that day.

The next hour went by in a blur. There were readings, and organ music filled the church. Father blessed the twins with holy water, then traced a cross in oil on their foreheads, followed by loads of pictures at the altar. Jo and Cole were being greeted by numerous people giving their congratulations and well wishes.

Meanwhile, Mitch and I still held the babies while the church janitor, Larry Turner, discreetly picked up in the background, readying the pews for the next event.

"Are you ready for all this?" I teased, not really certain I was actually joking. Nervous laughter slipped out of my mouth.

"Is something wrong?" Mitch scrunched his forehead into a deep V, and the scar along his jaw twitched beneath his five o'clock shadow. "You seem off, somehow. Troubled." He paused before adding, "Did I do something wrong?"

I was already shaking my head. "No, I promise you. It's not you, it's me."

He arched one black eyebrow high.

"That came out wrong." I laughed again. "We—as in you and me—are fine. It's just the April showers and this church and my mother..."

"I know it all can be intimidating, but everything will be okay, Tink." He gave me such a hopeful, comforting look as he added, "I promise *you*."

I inhaled a deep breath and tried for my best smile as I nodded.

"Ah, just the two I need to speak with." Father joined us back at the altar, still wearing his robes.

"Really?" I swallowed hard. "About what?"

"Well, unfortunately, we have a problem."

I gave Mitch a look that said, *I knew it!*

He tried not to roll his eyes, but I could tell it was a struggle.

"What seems to be the problem, Father?" Mitch asked.

"The problem is your date."

My stomach flipped. "Wait, we can't get married on May first?" Jeremiah started squirming and crying again, obviously feeling the panic within me. I plopped the pacifier back in his mouth, and it worked like a charm. Maybe I would have to get one for myself, I thought a little hysterically. I was finally getting everything I wanted, and my life was beginning to unravel.

"I'm not saying you can't get married on that date. I'm simply saying you can't get married in this church on that date." Father Comstock squeezed my shoulder. It was important to my mother that I get married at Sacred Heart by Father Comstock. She'd said as much, many times.

"Is it because we haven't been to church much?" Mitch asked, holding the other twin who was calm as can be, which only added to my stress that he would be a better parent than me. What had I been thinking?

"No, no, my child." Father patted my fiancé's shoulder. "I would like to see you both in church more often, but that's not the issue."

"Then what *is* the issue?" I kept my voice down because the church was still packed with most of the town after the twins' christening.

Father Comstock leaned forward and whispered, "I'm so sorry. I don't know how it happened, but your reservation was erased from our computer system. Someone else already has your date. Everything is already set for them, but if you want to choose another date, I'm sure we could work something out."

My face must have said it all.

"Yeah, that's not going to work, Father. You have no idea how long it took for Sunny to choose this date."

"Horoscopes don't lie, Father. We *have* to get married on May first. All the charts I consulted indicated that was the perfect date."

"Then you won't be having a church wedding, I'm afraid."

As if my mother had supersonic hearing, I felt the burn of her gaze in my back. Closing my eyes, I had serious doubts about my wedding for the first time.

Maybe it was a sign....

2

A week later, I stood in the back yard of Vicky, the ancient Victorian house I bought when I first moved to Divinity. This was the first break in the rain we'd had in days. The yard was huge and private, backing up to the woods. Cole was a carpenter and brought his supplies, insisting on making Mitch and me the most beautiful wooden arch for us to stand under during our wedding. The intricate details of vines and sunflowers and birds was breathtaking. He'd captured everything I love about the summer. I just wish the weather would cooperate with us. I really wanted an outdoor wedding.

"I still can't believe she can't get married in the church," my mother said from several feet away but definitely within earshot, which I was sure she was fully aware of. She was dressed in the latest designer fashion, with her hair styled perfectly chic. Meanwhile, I had on leggings and one of Mitch's old sweatshirts.

"Well, it certainly won't be traditional, but it's not the end of the world, Vivian," my father chimed in beside her, looking dapper as ever with his salt-and-pepper hair, Dockers, and Polo shirt. "With Judge

Harry performing the ceremony, everything will be just fine. You'll see. This probably suits Sunny better than a church anyway, given her profession and all. It's not very *holy*."

My parents loved me. They just had a hard time with me being a fortune teller, since I was their only child. As a former doctor and lawyer, they couldn't understand why my goals and aspirations weren't more like theirs. We'd learned to put our differences aside after they moved to Divinity and took over Divine Inspiration—the little inn on the outskirts of town—with their merry band of a misfit crew. At least they loved Mitch and were thrilled with the prospect of grandchildren.

Speaking of grands, my Granny Gert and her friend Great-Grandma Tootsie waddled into the back yard. Granny, with her snow-white hair and snappy brown eyes, wore her usual flour sack apron with a wooden spoon in the pocket as she carried a tray of her famous cookies. She stored them in a pumpkin cookie jar with a foil-covered plate on top since the lid broke years ago. She swore that was the secret.

Toots with the tight gray curls and faded blue eyes wore a checkered apron over her polyester pants, and carried a tray of gourmet sandwiches for everyone. You would never guess she was ninety-nine years old. She was as sharp as ever and still enjoyed a nightly rye and ginger. Maybe that was her secret.

Not to be outdone by anyone, Granny's nemesis-turned-BFF, Fiona, carried her famous pie, followed closely by her husband Harry, the ex-judge, who was no spring chicken himself as he was in his eighties. They were all retired and were the merry band of a misfit crew helping my parents at the inn.

"Thank goodness, ladies. You're Heaven-sent literal lifesavers." Jo handed her babies to the grannies, who all had open arms, and was the first to dig into the food.

My maid of honor was Jo, and Mitch's best man was Cole. Zoe and Sean were in the wedding as well. Zoe was a softer replica of Jo, and Sean was a blond-haired, blue-eyed reformed ladies' man with killer dimples. Sean went off to help Mitch and Cole, while Zoe joined Jo and me at the food buffet.

"We're all set with tables and chairs from the Legion. John Brown is going to bring them over next week," Zoe said while checking her clipboard. She was a party planner and had planned Jo's wedding, so I had asked her to plan mine.

"Who's that?" I asked.

"Local handyman. He does a bunch of stuff for everyone around town. I hired him to be my assistant and help me with the wedding plans. In fact, he managed to get a tent big enough for your back yard in case it rains."

"I owe him one."

"What if it's cold?" Jo asked. "April can still be quite chilly in upstate NY."

"I've got that covered." Zoe beamed. "Gas heat lamps strategically placed all around the reception space. With lanterns, fire pits, and seating areas clustered about, the whole theme will have to do with backyard BBQ's and summertime, even though it will still be Spring. A beautiful oasis of Mitch and Sunny's favorite things."

"I seriously don't know what I would do without you," I said. "I don't know why, but I feel like something is off."

"Oh, honey, do you remember what a mess I was?" Jo said between mouthfuls of food. She was nursing

Sasquatch twins and was starving all the time. "It's just cold feet. Completely normal."

"Then why doesn't Mitch have any?" I twisted my napkin between my hands, my gaze shooting over to my Detective Grumpy Pants, who hadn't been grumpy in far too long. He seemed way too calm, cool, and collected lately. Speak of the devil, his gaze caught mine and he winked. My insides melted. No matter what, he was always there for me, which made me feel even more guilty.

What was wrong with me?

He wanted to marry me, accepted what I did for a living *almost*, and had even agreed to me having our babies. Yet here I was the one with cold feet. I'd gone my whole life relying on my gut—my psychic intuition—and it had never steered me wrong. Something was off; I just wasn't sure what yet.

"Once Mitch makes up his mind about something, he's all in." Jo shrugged. "He had cold feet for a year. Now it's your turn."

"You're right. It's just cold feet, I guess. But if anything else goes wrong, I'm seriously going to lose it."

The rain started to fall once more at that moment. We all scrambled to grab everything that we could and make a mad dash inside my house. We made it just in time before the rain fell in sheets you could barely see through. Everyone sat around the long wooden harvest table, talking at once, while the Tasty Trio got to work taking over my kitchen, genuine root cellar and all.

Mitch lit the small fireplace in the corner and a teakettle sat atop the gas stove that had replaced the old coal-burning stove from years ago. There was a fancier large, round, dark wood table with pedestals out in the formal parlor, surrounded by overstuffed chairs made of leather, but no one used that much. We all seemed to prefer the coziness of this less formal part of the kitchen.

My cat, Morty, appeared from out of nowhere, per his usual style. He was big and pure white, with jet black eyes, wearing one of the bowties Granny Gert made for him. I'd never seen him eat or sleep; that's why I named him Morty—short for immortal. He held something in his mouth. Mitch must have seen him as well, because we both walked over to him at the same time.

"What is that?" Mitch asked, squatting down in front of Morty. They had always been rivals, fighting for my affection, but lately they had come to a truce of sorts. I think they both realized I wasn't going to choose between them, so they had better learn to get along if we all were going to live together in peace.

I reached out and took the object from my cat's mouth. "It looks like an old, rusted horseshoe. That's heavy. No normal cat would be able to carry that, but then again, Morty had never been normal." Mitch grunted, then I added, "I can't imagine why he would bring that home."

"He's a cat, though we all know he's much more than that. Still, cats bring home all sorts of things." Mitch shook his head and took the horseshoe from me and then carried it out the garage door to the trash can before returning to my side.

Morty stood, gave us a both an odd look, then turned and walked his snow-white tail regally out of the room as if bored with us. Everyone left the crowded kitchen and congregated in my living room for more space. Heavily upholstered, overstuffed chairs and sofa, sporting uniquely shaped and curved backs, sat polished and proud atop oriental rugs that covered the hardwood floors. Damasks, silks, and velvets covering every flat surface available were slightly dusty since Granny had moved into the inn with my parents. The draperies that dressed the stained-glass windows consisted of heavy fabrics in deep reds, greens, gold, and rich browns that blended beautifully as they hung over a lace underlining and were pulled back and secured with heavy cording and tassels. This was Morty's house, so I hadn't changed a thing, except my sanctuary where I did my readings.

A few moments later, a loud boom sounded that shook the house.

"Was that thunder?" I asked.

"It sure sounded like it," Cole said with a frown.

"I didn't see any lightning," Jo added.

"Is that smoke I smell?" my father asked.

My mother ran to the window that faced the backyard and gasped. "Call 911!"

"What? Why?" I shrieked, running to her side. "What happened?" I looked out back and let out a cry.

"What is it?" Harry asked, following us along with everyone else.

I took in all the faces staring at me and then turned my gaze on Cole. My heart fell as I answered, "The arch is on fire."

3

The next day I sat at the bar in Smokey Jo's Tavern, waiting for Zoe to arrive to go over more wedding plans. I should be filled with joy, but that niggling doubt in my gut wouldn't stop. First the mix-up with the church date, then the wedding arch burning down. What next? I couldn't help thinking these were signs that maybe we weren't supposed to get married. Mitch thought I was nuts, and insisted it was just a couple of unfortunate events. That it had nothing to do with bad luck or negative signs.

He wasn't the psychic. I was. I sipped a cup of tea and ate the tuna sandwich and French fries Jo had made me, pushing my doubts aside.

"I can't wait to see our dresses today. Zoe said the dry cleaner is finished with them." Jo clapped her hands from behind the mahogany bar.

Our local seamstress, Trixie Irving, was also the dry cleaner. My mother and I had been getting along better since she'd moved to Divinity. Who knew that is what it would take to repair our relationship? It also helped that I was wearing her wedding dress. Here I'd thought distance was the answer. As her only child, I had asked her if I could wear her dress. We didn't have the same taste in anything, and I had always been closer to and way more like my Granny Gert, but I knew my mother would be crushed if I wore Granny's dress instead of hers. She was too proud to ever ask me to wear it and risk being let down if I said no. So, I asked her. If it made her happy, then it made me happy.

"Trixie was able to alter your dress and Zoe's perfectly." I'd found them at the thrift store, much to my mother's horror, and they were perfect. "She had to let my mother's dress out to fit me. I guess there was just enough extra material along the seams to work, but if I gain a pound, I'm in trouble." Jo looked at the French fry dangling from my hand and giggled. I promptly set it down. "Anyway, all she had left to do was dry clean my mother's dress so I could try it on today."

"I'm here, I'm here. So sorry for being late," Zoe said as she joined us out of breath. "Cole is working on a new altar and keeping it at his construction yard under his watchful eye. It's even more beautiful, Sunny, I promise. It's funny, though. No one else in town heard lightning and thunder that night. Weird." She shrugged. "Anyway, I'm ready to go whenever you ladies are."

"You've got that right." Jo stood. "He won't even let *me* near it. The man isn't taking any more chances."

"You've got a good one, Jo. Don't let that one get away."

"Oh, don't you worry. He's not going anywhere. I worked too long and hard to get that man to see me as his wife. I'm not about to let him get away now that he said 'I do.' Besides, his Great Dane Biff loves me now, and he couldn't handle the twins on his own." She grinned and grabbed her keys.

Cole had been married once before, and his wife died on the back of his motorcycle. Jo had been friends with them both. It took a long time for Cole to open up his heart again, but he and Jo were so perfect for each other. That was all I wanted. To share my life with the man who had stolen my heart.

If only the pre-wedding chaos would stop.

A man in his thirties walked in wearing a baseball cap, sweatshirt, and jeans. He nodded to Zoe. "Trixie's ready for you now. I'm gonna grab a bite to eat and then help Sam fix his cooler. It's on the fritz, I guess."

"Oh, Sunny, this is John."

He smiled wide. "Ah, so you're the happy bride-to-be."

"That's me." I smiled back and shook his hand. "Thank you for all your help. It took me so long to pick a date and then I picked one that didn't give Zoe much time to plan the wedding. You've been a godsend."

"You're very welcome. I appreciate the extra work. I'll let you ladies get on with your day. It was nice to finally meet you."

"Same here. Maybe next time you can meet my fiancé, Mitch Stone."

"Looking forward to it." He tipped his hat and then headed for the bar.

Zoe and I followed Jo out the door and climbed into her truck. Five minutes later we pulled up in front of Irving's Iron and parked on the street. Once again it was raining as we went inside.

A middle-aged woman with black-and-gray streaked hair bustled over to us, full of energy. "I'm so excited, ladies. The dresses look spectacular."

"We can't wait to try them on," Zoe replied.

"Good, good. Follow me."

We walked into the back room and loads of clothes hung in plastic bags on hangers, ready to be picked up.

"This is my assistant, Darla Maple. She's new to town."

The woman looked to be in her mid-twenties, and up-to-date on the latest fashion by the way she was dressed and wore her hair. "It's so nice to meet you all. I love the dresses you picked out. Spring is my favorite time of year because of all the weddings."

We all welcomed her as Trixie pushed a button and the conveyor moved the clothes in a clockwise direction until she came to a certain section and she hit stop. The conveyor stopped and she pulled all of our dresses off the bar. She hung them on a rack and Darla wheeled them into the seamstress room where we could try them on, then step out on a platform in front of several mirrors situated where you could see every aspect of the gown.

Jo was up first. She disappeared behind a curtain and slipped on her dress. "Oh, my goodness, I'm going to cry."

"Oh, no, what's wrong?" Zoe asked.

Jo stepped out from behind the curtain and onto the platform. "Absolutely nothing," she managed to get out. "I look like the old me again instead of a tank, pregnant with Sasquatch babies."

"You are a vision of loveliness," I said, and meant it. The pale yellow dress fell in soft and simple waves over her perfect curves.

"I love it." Jo beamed.

"I'm glad." I smiled.

"You're up, Zoe." Trixie handed her another plastic-covered dress, while Jo went back behind the curtain to change.

Zoe snatched garment bag and quickly disappeared behind another curtain. "Oh, wow," she said moments later.

"Well, come on out here. We're dying to see," Jo said as she returned to her seat beside me.

Zoe stepped out from behind the curtain and onto the platform.

"Wow is right." My jaw fell open. I had chosen two yellow dresses but in vastly different styles. Jo's was soft and simple and lovely. Zoe's was silky and sexy and daring. If that didn't get Sean to propose, I didn't know what else would.

"You look gorgeous, Cuz." Jo's eyes glistened. "These hormones are killing me." She wiped a tear away.

"You both look amazing." I hugged her.

"And now it's time for the main attraction." Trixie grabbed the last garment bag and handed it to me. "Off you go."

My hands shook as I walked behind a special curtain reserved only for the bride. I had to admit I was starting to feel the excitement I should be feeling. I took a sip of champagne that waited for me on a side table. It was time I started letting myself enjoy the process. I deserved this. I unzipped the bag and stared at the front of my mother's gorgeous wedding dress. It was elegant and formal and cost a fortune. None of those things mattered to me, but I held onto the fact that my parents were still married and adored each other. Wearing her wedding dress had to be a good sign. And that was something I was in desperate need of.

I pulled the dress out and turned it around to unzip it, then screamed and dropped the garment on the floor.

"Sunny?"

"Are you okay?"

"What happened?"

All four women had appeared at my side in seconds, speaking at once.

"This." I turned the dress around and showed them the back.

Darla gasped and covered her mouth with both hands.

Trixie fainted straight away.

Zoe dropped to her side and fanned her face, then patted her cheeks.

Jo's face turned an alarming shade of purple. "This looks like the dress got caught in the machine and it chewed up the back."

"I'm pretty sure that's not fixable." I looked at Trixie who was now sitting up and looking wide eyed with horror.

"I have no idea when that happened."

"I could have sworn when I took it out and put it in the bag it was perfect," Darla said. "I don't know. We've been so busy lately, maybe I didn't notice the back, but I can't imagine not seeing that." She dropped her chin, and her shoulders wilted. "I am so very sorry. I'll pay for a new dress."

"It was my mother's dress from her wedding. It wouldn't be the same." I looked Trixie in the eye. "I know none of you meant for this to happen. It's just further proof."

"Of what?" Zoe asked.

"That something is off."

"What exactly are you trying to say, Sunny?" Jo asked, looking wary and a little fearful. Jo was my best friend, but she had known Mitch for far longer. She had a soft spot where he was concerned and didn't want to see him get hurt. Frankly, neither did I, but the signs could no longer be ignored.

"I'm saying what I've been saying, that no one seems to be listening to."

"And that is...?"

"This wedding is cursed."

4

_____

"I f one more thing happens, Mitch, I don't know what I'll do." I sipped my cocoa in the garage. It was the one area of Vicky in which Morty left Mitch alone. So Mitch had made it his man cave. Like my Sanctuary, where I did my fortune-teller readings, was my own personal space. We didn't bother each other in those spaces unless invited inside. Mitch had asked me to join him, so I did.

"You didn't really want to wear your mother's dress anyway. And she understands it getting stuck in the machine wasn't your fault." He tinkered with the engine on his motorcycle, wearing a pair of his old NYPD sweatpants and T-shirt. His black wavy hair was a mess, and his five o'clock shadow heavier than normal, almost fully covering the jagged scar on his jaw. He'd never looked more handsome to me than at that moment. He looked up and saw me watching him then quirked a brow. "What?"

I shrugged and took a sip before replying, "Oh, nothing. I just can't believe you're all mine."

He frowned, which wasn't the reaction I had been expecting. "Well, that's good. At least you're still attracted to me, so I guess there's hope."

I stood up and walked over to hug him. "I love you with all my heart, and I want nothing more than a future with you. I'm just not sure we have to say 'I do' in order to have that future. All the signs seem to be warning against a wedding. Can't we just live in sin?" I smiled wide and batted my eyelashes at him.

"Not a chance." He chuckled and shook his head. "Not long ago that would have been my line. We can't worry about signs, Sunny. We've had a streak of bad luck. That doesn't mean we shouldn't get married."

"Then maybe postpone the wedding?" I couldn't believe those words were coming out of my mouth.

"You spent a lot of time picking the perfect date. I'm not going to make you compromise on that because you're spooked."

"I can't explain it. I do believe we're perfect for each other, but something is off. This is more than a streak of bad luck. I can feel it."

"Yes, it's called cold feet, and it's completely normal."

"If you say so," I said, and finished my cocoa, looking around the garage. "You've really done a lot with this space."

"Thanks. It's finally feeling like my own."

I squinted by the side door. "Though I didn't expect you to decorate using the horseshoe Morty gave us."

Mitch's head snapped up. "I didn't. I threw that in the trash, remember? What are you talking about?"

"That." I pointed to the side door. "Over there."

Mitch walked over and picked up the horseshoe. "Well, I'll be." He shook his head then squinted as he studied the object closer. "I threw this out in the trash two days ago. That crazy cat is determined to give it to me. Don't know how he got it in here with the door closed. Then again, not much surprises me about Morty."

"Awww, that's so sweet." I walked over and joined him. "At least something good is happening. Horseshoes are for good luck. He must be trying to tell us he approves of us getting married."

Mitch picked up a hammer and nail and headed back to the door.

"What are you doing?"

"Not tempting fate." He laughed and proceeded to nail the horseshoe above the door.

I touched the horseshoe for good luck. My head whipped back and vision narrowed into tunnel vision like it always did when I was picking up a reading. I was brought back decades in time as I looked through the dark eyes of an elderly man with snow white hair, a top hat, and a bowtie. I was at the horse races in Saratoga Springs during the Kentucky Derby. Ladies wore huge, elaborate hats and drank mint julips, while the men all looked dapper in their Sunday best. People cheered their favorite horses on, having a grand old time, when the same niggling feeling settled in my stomach.

Something was off.

Just then the phone rang, jarring me out of my vision. I let go of the horseshoe and shook my hand. It felt like it had burned me. When I touched it again, nothing happened. The vision was gone. What on earth could it have meant, and who was that man? He seemed so familiar to me.

"You okay?" Mitch asked.

I nodded, so he answered his phone in full detective mode. His face grew serious, then he glanced at me for a moment before hanging up.

"Who was that?"

"Detective Fuller." Mitch rubbed his jaw and gnawed at the inside of his cheek. I'd known him long enough to know that wasn't a good sign. "Where did you say Zoe ordered our wedding cake from?"

"Sam's Bakery." I frowned. "Why?"

"The health department just shut them down after rats were found inside."

"Rats?" My heart sank. "Come on. What next? We both know how clean Sam is. I'm telling you—our wedding is cursed."

"Our wedding is not cursed, but I do think you're right about one thing."

"What's that?"

"Something is definitely up, all right, and it doesn't have anything to do with signs." Detective Grumpy Pants was back in full force. "We are *not* changing our date. Someone is trying to sabotage our wedding, and more than their feet will be cold by the time I'm through with them."

5

"Hey, guys, what's up?" Detective Juan Torres asked as he took a seat at the table with Mitch and me in Warm Beginnings & Cozy Endings Café. It was an inviting and homey café with a cream swirled floor and lots of charm. The owner Natalie Kirsch brought Juan over his usual black coffee. He'd only been to town a handful of times, but she never forgot anyone's order, even strangers, due to her photographic memory.

Juan used to be Mitch's partner in the Homicide Division in New York City before Mitch left and became a small-town detective in Divinity. Juan eventually did the same, one town over in Salvation. Mitch often wondered if Juan resented him for abandoning him, but Juan said he understood. After Mitch's little sister died because a criminal wanted revenge, Mitch had never been able to forgive himself. He'd raised her after his parents died and couldn't help feeling like he'd let everyone down. That was one of the reasons he didn't want children. I had changed his mind, but that didn't mean he wasn't still scared to death he would let me down as well. Even though now I was the one terrified of doing exactly that.

"Sunny's having cold feet," Mitch said point blank.

"You're kidding?" Juan's dark eyes grew wide, turning on me with questions.

"I'm not having cold feet, really. They're just a little chilled." I couldn't explain the bad feeling in my gut without sounding crazy. The problem was my gut never lied, and the vision I'd just had confirmed that something was most definitely off.

"You two are crazy about each other, that much is obvious." Juan studied us both, then looked directly at me. "Last I heard you wanted the whole package, white picket fence, babies and all."

"That's what I thought, too." Mitch scrubbed a hand over his messy hair, looking more tired and strained than I'd seen him in a long time.

"I'm not saying I still don't. There are just too many negative signs that say getting married right now might not be a good idea." I played with the tea bag in my half-empty cup, knowing I risked losing Mitch all together by backing out now after I'd taken so long to even set a date.

"There aren't any signs saying we shouldn't get married." Mitch's jaw hardened. "Too many things have happened for this to be a coincidence. Someone is obviously trying to sabotage our wedding. The question is who and why?"

"Agreed. Things do look a little suspicious based on what you told me." Juan looked at Mitch. "My question is, why me? Why not get the help from your department?"

"Mayor Cromwell adores Sunny but doesn't really care for me," Mitch said.

"You're like a son to Chief Spencer, and he isn't exactly a fan of mine," I responded.

"The only one on our side in rooting for this wedding to take place is Captain Walker," Mitch added, "but he likes to keep the peace around the precinct so I can't see him taking sides. Basically, I'm out of options."

"What about Detective Fuller?"

"The wedding is only a couple weeks away. Fuller is too busy eating donuts and working other cases to be much help." Mitch rolled his eyes.

"All right then, I'm all yours." Juan held up his empty mug to Natalie, then pulled out his notebook. "Bring me up to speed."

Before we could jump in, Larry, the church maintenance man, approached our table. He was a middle-aged, average man who was fairly new to town and mostly kept to himself, which was why I was surprised he went out of his way to speak with us. I had always meant to reach out and be more welcoming, but life had gotten in the way. I would have to do better. He was probably lonely.

"I just want to apologize for the mix-up at the church," he said. "It really was a shame. I'm there pretty much all the time and never saw anything suspicious. I heard about all the other things going wrong, too. Everyone in town has. I'm rooting for you both to get what you deserve." He nodded, smiled a little, then left without another word.

"Friend of yours?" Juan asked, staring after the man.

"Not really. He's just a little different," I said. "I'll have to bring him some of Granny's cookies next week."

"Back to our case," Mitch said. "The first thing that happened is the computer mix-up with the church giving away our wedding date. Divinity's townsfolk are pretty simple. Not computer savvy by any means, except for one individual." Mitch shot me a glance with a raised brow. "You care to tell him, Tink, or should I?"

"Sure thing, Detective Grumpy Pants." I rolled my eyes at him this time and then focused my attention on Detective Torres. "His name is Winston Penfield. He just graduated from high school. I gave him a reading, which revealed he had a bright future ahead of him. I gave him everything I saw, but he interpreted the clues wrong. He passed up a job at an up-and-coming tech company to work for a cyber security company. Unfortunately, the security company proceeded to downsize almost immediately after hiring him, and he lost his job. When he reached back out to the tech company once more, they had already filled the position. Now he blames me for steering him wrong." I was psychic, and my visions always came true, but it sometimes took a while to figure out exactly what a reading meant. I couldn't control how others interpreted what I said.

Juan made a note. "Anything else?"

"Karen Rogers," I said, looking Mitch straight in the eye. "You care to tell him, or should I?"

The corners of Mitch's mouth twitched with obvious amusement. He loved sparring with me. Looking at Juan, he said, "So, the second thing that happened is the wedding arch Cole built for us burned down. We all thought it was due to thunder and lightning, but no one else heard any thunder or saw any lightning that night. Upon closer inspection, Fire Chief Linda Drummond said it was arson. Karen Rogers is a former park ranger. Ironically, she lost her job after getting busted for setting fires when she was supposed to be preventing them."

"What does she have to do with you?" Juan eyed

Mitch with interest and a fair amount of his own amusement.

"*He* is the officer who busted her," I gladly chimed in. "Turns out she had a crush on him and kept setting little fires she could control so he would come and investigate, except one got away from her and nearly burned down Mini Central Park."

"Well, that certainly gives a whole new meaning to the one that got away." Torres chuckled. "I can't imagine she's too happy with you."

"Ya *think*?" Mitch grunted. "Moving on," he added firmly. "When the dry-cleaning machine broke and shredded Sunny's wedding dress, Trixie was beside herself. She said she had just had it serviced that day by Dawson Jones. He used to work for Big Don's Auto, and worked on Sunny's VW Bug many times."

"And...?" Juan looked up when Mitch paused.

"Well, Sunny shot him down hard," Mitch responded, whistling while motioning his hand like an airplane falling, then crashing and burning, ending with an explosion sound.

He was enjoying himself a little too much for my liking.

"You know my radar is horrible when it comes to men. I had no idea he was trying to ask me out." I scowled at Mitch. "What are you, five?"

He winked at me.

"Okay, children, do I have to put you both in a time-out?"

"Knowing my fiancé, he would probably like that way too much."

"Only if you go in the time-out with me." His smile turned tender, and everything in me softened.

Juan just laughed and shook his head. "Anything

else I should know before I leave you lovebirds alone?"

"The last thing that happened is after touching a horseshoe Morty brought home, I had a strange vision that gave me a feeling of doom moments before Sam's Bakery got shut down for a rat infestation," I said. "Sam was supposed to make our wedding cake."

"Yeah, rats and Sam are two words no one would ever put together in the same sentence. Sam is a freak about keeping his bakery clean and is furious because now his reputation is on the line." Mitch checked his notes. "Al Winters is a rival baker who always comes in second in any contest to do with Sam. Sabotage might be a real possibility."

"Maybe. I'll look into it." Juan closed his notebook. "I have another lead I'd like to follow as well. I'll fill you in on the details later."

"Thanks, buddy, we really could use an objective perspective. We'll look into things on our end as well, we're just neck-deep in wedding plans. It's hard to juggle it all."

"I've got your back, just like old times." He smiled, but his eyes looked a little sad. "I miss you, bro."

"Same here." Mitch fist pumped Juan.

A part of me wondered if he was bored with small-town life. Maybe they both longed for the big city again. Would Mitch come to regret marrying me someday? My stomach turned over once more.

And just like that, my feet grew colder.

6

"Come on, Winston, admit it. You were mad at me so you tried to sabotage my wedding by hacking into the church computer," I said as I stood at the front desk in the computer lab of Divinity Community College. After getting laid off from the security company and with no position left at the tech company, he had gotten a job in the computer lab of the community college. Not exactly his dream job to say the least.

Winston pushed his glasses further up his pointy nose, his beady brown eyes narrowing. "You ruined my life, but that doesn't mean I would waste a single thought on you. I don't care about your stupid wedding."

"I didn't ruin your life. I can't help it you interpreted the reading I gave you wrong," I responded. "You're the only one in town who would know how hack into a computer. It had to be you." I glanced around, realizing we weren't alone and several eyes were staring at us, including Larry. He waved, and I blinked, then waved back. Leaning in toward Winston, I lowered my voice. "You can tell me. I can put in a good word so you don't get into as much trouble. I just really need to know the truth."

He smoothed a hand over his perfectly side-parted Ken doll hair and puffed out his chest. "If I wanted to, I could mess with the entire town's computers, but that doesn't mean that I did. Besides, I have an alibi. I was with my mother on the day that the hacking happened. You can ask her."

I held my hands up, completely baffled. "There's no way to know when the computer was hacked into."

He leaned forward this time and shot me a smug look, making it clear he was way smarter than me. "Yes, there is. Just because things are deleted from a computer doesn't mean they're gone forever. Files can be recovered and hacking activity can be traced. I already did that for Detective Stone. You might want to talk to your *fiancé* before harassing me."

"I'm not harassing you." I took a deep, calming breath, realizing questioning him alone was a bad idea. "I'm simply questioning you."

"On what authority? Last I checked, you weren't employed by the Divinity Police Department."

"Look, I'm just trying to figure out what happened." I tried to appeal to his sense of humanity. "My future is at stake." As soon as the words left my mouth, I realized they probably weren't the best choice.

His face flushed. "Yeah, so was mine and look how that turned out."

"I'm sorry things didn't work out for you. I truly am. I'm sure there will be other opportunities that come your way, I'm sure. I can feel it. I could give you another reading for free this time if that would help." His face hardened, so I slid my card on the desk in front of him before he could say a word. "If you can think of anything else that might be helpful, please give me a call."

He ripped the card up right in front of me and threw it in the trash. "Good day, Ms. Meadows. I have work to do."

Well, that was a waste of time, I thought, as I stepped out of the campus computer lab into a light drizzle. I was really beginning to dislike the month of April. I pulled up the hood of my raincoat and started walking to my well-loved VW Bug with orange, yellow, and pink flowers on the sides. The car suited me perfectly, even though she didn't always work the best, which had me thinking of Dawson Jones.

Dawson was very similar in looks and build to my fiancé, which was probably why Mitch didn't even like bringing up his name. I hadn't even known Dawson was flirting with me back then. Mitch was worried that if I had known, I might have said yes to Dawson before Mitch could ask me out. I reassured Mitch that I loved him for much more than his looks, but he still got jealous.

Could Dawson really have tried to sabotage our wedding because he was jealous as well? Or maybe he was just angry at me for unknowingly shooting him down? He was the last one to fix the dry-cleaning machine before my wedding dress was shredded. He'd certainly had access to the gown alone. Darla had said the dress had looked fine the last she saw it. Maybe he had taken out his frustrations by ruining it when no one was watching. That seemed rather petty, given it had been over a year since the incident between us.

Maybe I would go have a little chat with Dawson now before Mitch found out. That wouldn't exactly go over well if he knew. He tended to be overly protective of me and didn't like when the police used me as a consultant. Although, he had started to come around in his belief of my abilities as well as working with me. That was the key. He preferred to work with me rather than have me go rogue and work on my own. Even I had to admit trouble seemed to follow me when I worked alone.

Besides, Mitch couldn't get mad because he'd already talked to Winston on his own and hadn't shared what he'd found out, making me look like a fool in front of Mr. Smarty Pants. Mitch knew I was stressed about the wedding, so he was probably trying to solve this mystery for me. If we'd learned anything over the past year, it was that keeping things from each other never worked out well. We needed to work together, and I would do exactly that just as soon as I finished with Dawson.

I was halfway across the parking lot, when I felt the hairs on the back of my neck prickle. I froze and listened, but I didn't hear anything. Peeking over my shoulder, I didn't see anything, either. So, I started walking again. This time I picked up my pace. All of my senses came alive as I felt eyes burning into my back. Were those footsteps I heard? I spun around in a circle but still didn't see anything.

Something or someone was out there.

I was certain of it. I could sense the tension in the air. The rain picked up, wind whipping across the pavement, and I jogged the last few yards until I reached my Bug. My hand shook as I fished the keys out of my pocket, and I dropped them when I tried to put them in the lock. My heartbeat sped up as I bent over to pick them up. I froze once more. I felt a strong sensation of a powerful presence right behind me. I whipped around in a squatting position, holding the keys in my fist like a weapon, and screamed, falling back on my butt.

"Morty!" Relief shot through me replaced quickly by anger. "You scared me half to death. Don't do that again, please." I frowned. "Is that what I think it is?" I took from Morty's mouth the same rusted horseshoe that Mitch had hung on the wall, but I wasn't picking up any readings. I could feel strong energy coming from it, but that was it.

Standing up, I opened my car door and Morty jumped into the passenger seat. Usually, he appeared and disappeared at will and never let me drive him anywhere. Whenever I was in trouble, he always showed up to protect me. Well, that settled that. Guess I wouldn't be seeing Dawson today. Morty was trying to tell me something, but once more, I wasn't sure exactly what.

A chill trickled down my spine as the feeling of being watched returned. Morty stared intensely into my eyes, and for once I understood exactly what he meant. I quickly slid into the driver's seat then shut and locked my door. I headed straight for home with one thought racing through my mind...

I had an enemy in this town, and they weren't done with me yet.

7

"I hope you're okay with this, Mother," I said as I stood in the living room of Divine Inspiration, modeling Granny Gert's wedding dress.

I adored vintage clothing. This one was a simple, elegant, A-line sleeveless satin dress with a bow on the back. It came to my knees and the skirt was sheer with satin trim layered over a satin underskirt. A pair of white satin pumps were the perfect accessory.

"Well, it's not my gown, but even I have to admit, this one suits you perfectly." Her eyes softened as she looked at me. "You look beautiful, darling."

"Thanks, Mom." I gave her a hug. Now that the dress fiasco was fixed and my mother was okay with it, the women all started talking at once.

"Well, bless my stars, you look just like me," Granny Gert said while hopping up and down in her seat.

"Boys oh day, you look like an angel," Great-Grandma Tootsie started humming show tunes and clapping her hands.

"Oh, my word, you are a vision, my dear," Fiona clapped her cheeks with her palms, nodding and getting misty-eyed at the same time.

"Thank you, ladies," I said, twirling around once. "I feel like a princess."

"Here," Jo said, coming to stand behind me. She fastened a short veil to the back of my head and pulled the netting over my face. It came to a stop at my chin. "Now, that's perfect, just like you."

"Oh, my gosh! Sunny, you look amazing." Zoe came in with John beside her. He was staying at the inn until he found a house.

"Wow, you look beautiful, Ms. Meadows." He pulled the baseball cap off his head and fiddled with it, his cheeks flushing slightly.

"Thank you both. I'm finally feeling like a bride."

"Everything's going smoothly, I promise," Zoe said, then turned to John. "Can you take care of that thing we talked about today?"

He pulled his cap back on and nodded once, looking relieved to be leaving all the girly things. "No worries, boss. I'm off to take care of that right now."

"I don't know how I would have pulled all this off without him," Zoe said. "And Darla felt so bad, she has been amazing, helping me out in her spare time as well. In fact, they're both single and I'm starting to think they might be sweet on each other." She beamed.

My mother and the grannies and Fiona had all gotten back to work, so it was just Zoe, Jo, and me left in the room.

"Awww, that's sweet. I'm glad you have help after I sprung it on you so quickly. With all the chaos happening, it can't be easy. Mitch thinks someone's trying to sabotage the wedding. I took it all as negative signs that we shouldn't get married, but I'm beginning to think he's right. That was no storm that burned down the arch. The fire chief ruled it as arson."

"Well, don't you worry," Jo said. "No one is touching the new one Cole made, and it's even more spectacular than the last one. I just can't believe anyone would be against you two getting married. Do you have a clue who it might be?"

I filled them in on all the suspects we had. "Now that Winston is ruled out, there's only Karen Rogers, Dawson Jones and Al Winters left. Mitch won't let me near Dawson, so he's going to go talk to him today. Care to pay a visit to Karen Rogers with me?"

"I'm free," Jo said. "Cole is watching the twins to give me a break."

"I would, but there are too many things I still have left to do," Zoe said, "including a little surprise I have for you."

"I heard when you were talking to John," I said, having always been a fan of surprises. My fiancé, on the other hand, hated anything he couldn't control. I mostly wanted to know what it was for his sake. "Can't you give me a hint?"

"Then it wouldn't be a surprise, now, would it?" Mischief sparkled from her amber eyes, and she headed out the door without another word.

Ten minutes later, I was changed and on the road with Jo.

"Where are we going?" I asked. Jo was driving again, as usual. She was another one who loved to be in control.

"The zoo." Jo turned down a road that led to the outskirts of town.

"I love animals, too, but we don't have time for that."

Jo laughed at me. "That's where Karen Rogers works, you nut."

"Oh," I giggled, too, feeling good to release a little

tension. "I guess I've been in my own little world lately. I've been so busy with the wedding—the last reading I did was for Mayor Cromwell a week ago. He's a regular, along with Gary from the hardware store, but I can't even focus on them. I canceled the rest of my appointments until this wedding is over with, if it even happens."

"It will," Jo said with determination. "You'll see."

We pulled into the parking lot of the zoo and got out. For once, it wasn't raining. One of the first dates I had with Mitch was here. He knew how much I loved animals. I smiled fondly, realizing Mitch was always doing special little things to please me. We hadn't been here in a long time, though.

We each bought a ticket and made our way inside. There was an indoor exhibit with all sorts of reptiles, birds, and fish. Then there was an outdoor exhibit for all the other animals. We came to the elephant exhibit and finally found Karen. We sat through her show, which I had to admit was informative and interesting. After it finished, people asked questions and then finally made their way on to the next exhibit. Jo and I walked up to the gate just as Karen turned around.

The smile vanished from her face, turning into a scowl. "Oh, no you don't. You two aren't about to accuse me of arson. I've heard all about your string of bad luck. I did my time and paid the ultimate price in losing my dream job. All for a man who couldn't care less."

"Detective Stone is a good man, Karen. He was only doing his job," I said, crossing my arms over my chest and standing my ground. I wasn't about to let her talk bad about my fiancé. He didn't deserve that just because she was obsessed with him enough to break the law.

"Yeah, well, that's ancient history. I've moved on, as you can see. I might not be a park ranger, but I have an important job with these magnificent animals. They look gentle, but trust me, if you back them into a corner, they will fight back." A gust of wind kicked up dust in their enclosure. Suddenly it didn't sound like we were talking about elephants.

"Where were you the night of the storm, anyway?" Jo asked.

"I wasn't even in town. I was visiting my boyfriend. He's a real man." She looked at me smugly. "Like I said, I've moved on."

"You can verify this, of course," Jo said dryly.

"Naturally." She wiped her hands on her pants. "If we're done here, I have more important things to do."

I nodded once, and she left, post haste.

"Well, that was worth a whole lot of nothing," I said, as we headed toward the entrance, when I noticed a woman taking pictures by the wolf enclosure. "What is Darla doing here?" I asked.

"Maybe she's on a date with John," Jo said.

"Let's go talk to her." I started walking in that direction, weaving my way through the crowd. The zoo was busy that day.

We had almost reached her when we saw Karen stop and talk to her. Their heads were bent close together. Karen looked up as if sensing our presence, then she straightened her spine after spotting us and walked away in the other direction. A group of teenagers swarmed in front of us. By the time they moved on, Darla was gone.

"Interesting," Jo said.

"Exactly." We headed for the gate once more. "Maybe this trip wasn't a total bust after all."

8

---

itch picked me up the next day and we headed to Sam's Bakery. "I still don't like that bruise that's forming on your cheek. How did you get it again?"

"I ran into a wall." He looked straight ahead as he drove. "Mechanic shops can be dangerous places."

"Right. And this has nothing to do with a certain mechanic named Dawson Jones?" I stared him down, but he still refused to meet my eyes.

"Dawson refused to talk or cooperate. Said he fixed the machine and left, and I couldn't prove otherwise. Someone is obviously still sore over losing you." A muscle in Mitch's jaw bulged as he added, "I left and hit a wall on my way out. End of story."

"I bet you did," I responded, knowing that was definitely not the end of the story, but also knowing I would get nowhere if I pushed the subject of Dawson Jones.

"Al Winters isn't even in town. I sure hope we have more luck with Sam," Mitch changed the subject.

Smart man.

We parked and knocked on the door. Sam let us inside.

"Hey, guys, I really am so sorry about your cake. I'm still in shock." His face turned purple he was so angry. "This is my reputation. Anyone who knows me, knows how clean I keep my kitchen."

"We know," I said. "It's okay, Sam. Granny Gert is going to make her cookies, Fiona is making her famous pies, and Great-Grandma Tootsie is making the food. We've got everything covered. I just feel horrible you've been involved in all this."

"All this?"

"Someone is trying to sabotage our wedding, and we're trying to find out who and why," Mitch said gravely.

Sam's eyes widened. "I had no idea."

"Can you walk us through what happened?" Mitch pulled out his notebook, in full detective mode now.

I did the same, which always amused him somehow.

"At first I thought Al Winters was behind the rats. He comes in second place in any contest we're both entered, so I thought for sure he was trying to ruin me. Turns out he's not even in town. Plus, Detective Fuller said the rats weren't even normal rats."

Mitch and I glanced at each other. "What do you mean, not normal?" he asked.

"I guess they are from the local pet store. Elaina Sands said someone broke into her store and stole the rats. She reported it to Fuller."

Maybe not including Mitch's department had been a bad idea. We hadn't heard a word from Detective Torres, when apparently, we should have been checking in with Detective Fuller all along.

"John fixed my freezer, but the health department hasn't cleared me to officially re-open yet. I've lost so much business, this had better not ruin me."

"I'm sure it won't. Like you said, anyone who knows you, knows how clean you are and how amazing your baked goods are. I'm really sorry this happened to you."

"Thank you." Sam nodded gravely. "Same to you."

We said our goodbyes and headed for home.

"Why do you think Juan hasn't updated us? It seems strange," I said.

Mitch gnawed the inside of his cheek. "That's a good question. Maybe it's time we found out."

As we left Sam's Bakery, I couldn't help but do a double take. Larry the maintenance man pulled into the exact spot we were parked and walked up to the door. Sam let him inside, which had me wondering what on earth they could be meeting about.

Ten minutes later, we pulled in the driveway of our house. Mitch headed straight for the garage. Torres was supposed to meet him there in half an hour to fill him in on what he was up to. I decided they needed their space in case they had issues to resolve. I hopped in my VW Bug and headed toward Mini Central Park.

It was another non-rainy day. I missed the sunshine, craved feeling the warm rays on my face. The temperatures were mild today, and every ounce of my being needed to be outside. So I drove to one of my favorite places, the park in the center of town with our resident swans, Fred and Ginger. I climbed out of my Bug and walked over to the footbridge that crossed the pond. A sudden feeling of being watched swept over me again. I glanced around but didn't see anything. I was beginning to think my mind was playing tricks on me. I hadn't told anyone where I was going, but it had been a while since any murders had taken place. I needed to relax and stop worrying. Allow myself to enjoy this rare moment of good weather.

Breaking off pieces of bread I'd had in my car, I threw them out to the trumpeting swans. "Ladies first, Fred," I hollered, smiling as I pictured Granny Gert. She loved the swans. I had to admit, I missed her since she'd moved in with my parents, but they needed her more than I did these days. Guess it was time I grew up and moved on with my life. With my new husband. I swallowed hard, still having doubts. So many things had gone wrong. What if it really was signs from the universe and not sabotage? I didn't know what to think anymore.

After an hour of pondering, I decided I'd given Mitch and Juan enough space. It was the end of April, so the days were still short and the sun still went down fairly early. Dusk was setting, and I didn't want to get stuck out here alone. I headed back to my car and climbed inside. Turning the key, nothing happened. I turned it again, still nothing.

Dead battery.

I picked up my phone and groaned. How could I have let my phone die as well? Mitch was going to have a fit. If I walked, it would be pitch black before I got home. I got out and popped the hood, then looked around.

A man walked toward me in the shadows, and I had to practice my deep breathing not to hyperventilate. "Ms. Meadows?" Larry said, emerging from the shadows. "What are you doing here?"

"I could ask you the same thing." I laughed nervously, scanning my surroundings for anything to use as a weapon.

"I like to come here to think. I've got to admit I didn't expect to see anyone else." He looked at my raised hood. "Car trouble?"

"No, I'm good, I was just checking the oil." I put the

top down.

"Well, I'll wait here and make sure you get going okay."

"That's really not necessary."

He gave me the strangest look. "Trust me, it is. Dark woods are no place to be when the sun goes down."

A car pulled up just then. John and Darla sat in the front and he rolled down the window, looking between Larry and me. "You okay, Ms. Meadows?"

"Actually, no. My car won't start." Larry's eyes cut to mine, but I ignored his penetrating look. "Would you mind giving me a ride?"

"Sure thing." He got out and raised my hood to check a few things. "Probably a dead battery by the sound of it. I'll get you home, then call for a tow to Big Don's. You sure you don't want me just to call Mitch now?"

"No, definitely not." I wasn't up for a lecture right now.

"I can give you a ride, Ms. Meadows," Larry chimed in.

"No," I said a little too quickly. "I mean, John and Darla already offered." I rushed around to the other side of the truck, but Darla was already in the back seat.

"You can sit in the front. John has way too much junk back here." She laughed, and he just shrugged.

"Comes with the territory of being a jack-of-all-trades. Never know what job I'll get called for next." He shut the door behind me and then walked around to climb into the front seat of his truck. He nodded to Larry, who just kept staring at me with such intense eyes, they were unnerving.

We pulled out of the parking lot, and I felt like I
had just dodged a bullet.

9

J ohn pulled onto the main road and headed toward town. "I have to get gas," he said over my confused expression.

"Thank you so much, you have no idea how scared I was," I said.

"Why?" Darla asked.

"Larry was giving me the creepiest vibes. If you guys hadn't shown up, I don't know what would have happened. I really do appreciate it."

"No worries." We pulled into the gas station and John filled the tank.

Five minutes later we were back on the road, heading toward my house. We saw police lights up ahead. John slowed the truck as we passed by. Mitch and Juan were both on the side of the road, questioning Larry. I made eye contact with Larry, who still stared at me in an unnerving way.

"Do you want me to stop?" John asked.

"Good Lord, no!" I ducked. "Mitch is going to be so mad. I'm just glad they caught Larry. I felt bad for him, thinking he was just lonely. Obviously, I judged him wrong." I sat back up a moment later. "Wait, you missed the turn. This is the wrong way." I reached out and touched John's arm.

Just like that I was pulled into tunnel vision. I was looking through the eyes of a man with a trunk full of drugs. My breathing was choppy and my heart was racing. I was staring at the barrel of a gun. The next thing I knew I was in handcuffs and then behind bars. Rage and hatred filled my being as I counted the days, months, years that went by. Finally, I was free. Free but I couldn't forget or forgive or move on. I returned to my ways, moving from town to town, looking for all sorts of jobs. I could do almost anything, a jack of all trades.

For a while, life was okay. But then I saw him. All the pent-up rage and hate returned. I couldn't let him get away with what he had done to me. He had stolen my happiness. He certainly didn't deserve to be happy himself. I was on a computer, then I was buying flammable liquids, then I had a wrench in my hand, then I was breaking and entering and stealing something that wiggled.

"Ms. Meadows? Sunny?" Darla's voice yanked me back to reality.

I stared at John with my mouth open.

He finally turned in my direction, recognition dawning. "I heard you were psychic. Guess I didn't really believe it." He shot me a sinister grin. "Until now."

"It was you all along, wasn't it?"

"What are you talking about?" Darla asked. "John, what does she mean?"

He smirked into the rearview mirror at Darla. "She means I'm not really John Brown." His gaze hardened and turned on me with all the rage and hate I had just felt. "The name's Chance LeRoy. Your fiancé busted me for drugs years ago. Ruined my life."

Darla gasped. "What? But I thought we—"

"We aren't anything more than a distraction, darlin'. My main focus has and always will be on getting my revenge. Detective Stone and his sidekick Torres stole my happiness. I'll be damned if I'll let them find happiness of their own. I never imagined the gift that would land in my lap when I moved to Divinity. Your fiancé and his old partner have gotten soft. Stone has seen me countless times but has never put two and two together. My hair's longer and I have a beard now, but still. I can't believe he hasn't recognized me yet."

"What exactly do you plan to do with me?" I asked.

"I didn't plan to do anything with you except ruin your wedding. But now that you know who I am and all the things I've done, I can't let you go."

"So, you're going to murder her?" Darla squeaked.

"Babe, my hands are tied. I'm going to have to kill you both. You were a nice distraction, but I can't risk either of you talking. I have big plans, a gig that will set me up for life."

"We're not going to die, Darla," I said, giving John or Chance or whoever his name was a hard glare. "You have no idea whom you're messing with."

"Detective Stone doesn't scare me."

"I'm not talking about him."

"Torres is hardly a threat."

"Not talking about him, either."

His gaze shot to mine, looking wary for the first time. "You might be psychic but you're not exactly a threat. A little slip of a woman like you can't take me in a fight."

"You don't know what I'm capable of when my back's against the wall, but I'm not talking about me, either."

"Then what are you talking about?"

"My cat, Morty."

He let out a barking laugh over that one. "You can't be serious."

"Deadly so."

"I'm shaking in my boots, lady." He shook his head, still laughing, and looked back at the road, then his eyes widened as the air seemed to be sucked out of his lungs. An eerily glowing white form sat in the middle of the road with razor sharp fangs bared, and John shouted, "What the...?" He swerved at the last second and we veered off the road, crashing into a tree.

My seatbelt locked and the airbags went off, slamming me against the seat. My neck was sore, and every ounce of my being hurt. "Darla?" I called out.

"I'm okay. I had my seatbelt on, too."

A moan came from beside me. I looked at John, and he was slumped over the steering wheel. He hadn't worn his seatbelt, his head smashing into the windshield before the airbag pushed him back into his seat. He moaned again as sirens sounded off in the distance. "What the heck was that?" he mumbled.

I looked at him with disgust as I answered, "*That* was Morty."

It felt like hours but I knew it was only a matter of minutes. Help had arrived. John aka Chance was hauled away in an ambulance, but he would be going back to jail for sure. Darla was being taken to the hospital in a different ambulance to get checked out, and I sat at the back of a third ambulance where Mitch held my hand and cast worried stormy grey eyes at me.

"I still can't believe John Brown was really Chance LeRoy," I said in wonder.

"That was the lead Detective Torres had been following when I asked for his help," Mitch responded.

"What shocked me was that Larry was really an undercover FBI agent. If you hadn't driven by, we wouldn't have known where Chance was taking you. Larry knew there was no way Chance would let you go once you knew who he was. He'd been tailing him for some time and knew all his hideouts. We followed his hunch and found you on this back road."

"Morty found me too." I had to acknowledge my feline hero as well.

"Somehow that cat always seems to beat me to the scene." Mitch chuckled, and my heart swelled. "Now do you see I was right? Our wedding isn't cursed at all."

And just like that, I saw a flash of white light in the nearby trees and the knot which had been gnawing at my insides suddenly disappeared. A smile stretched so wide across my face my cheeks hurt. "Never better." I saw recognition in his eyes at my underlying meaning.

"No more curses, no more sabotage, no more cold feet, just me and you." He winked.

"And Morty." I blew him a kiss.

He nodded then arched an inquisitive and sexy as all get out brow. "So... we're good, Tink?"

"Oh, we're *very* good, Detective," I said, still smiling.

Mitch wrapped me in his arms. "Then I suggest we get you home and make you a married woman."

For the first time in weeks, I felt the genuine excitement a bride should be feeling. And I owed it all to my grumpy detective.

EPILOGUE

"**Y**ou may now kiss your bride," Judge Harry said with a fond smile on his face.

Mitch took me in his arms, dipped me backwards, and kissed me square on the lips. Everyone whooped and hollered as he picked me up and twirled me around in a dizzying circle before setting me back on my feet. The rain had stopped the night before, the sun shining bright on our special day with the most beautiful rainbow arching over us.

"I give to you for the very first time, Mr. and Mrs. Stone," Harry added, and we turned to face the crowd gathered under the massive tent in Vicky's backyard.

Mitch and I stepped out from under the gorgeous arch Cole had built for us and greeted our guests. The entire town was there. Both my parents had given me away, Great-Grandma Tootsie had cooked the food, Granny Gert made an assortment of cookies, and Fiona had made her famous pies. Zoe had surprised me with picture boards, while Darla had created a slide show of all the favorite places Mitch and I had gone on dates. Turns out Darla had only been talking to Karen because she asked her to create a flyer for an upcoming event at the zoo. Nothing more. Darla dabbled in other forms of design than just fashion.

Sean had surprised us all by proposing to Zoe on the dance floor.

After hours of dancing, the last of our guests finally left, leaving me alone for the first time with my husband. My head spun with dizzy happiness over the thought that this complicated, grumpy, passionate, loyal, thoughtful, amazing man was mine. Once I realized all the chaos had nothing to do with me, all of my doubts went away. We sat in front of a cozy fire on the couch, curled up together with champagne.

Even Morty had made himself scarce.

Mitch stared at the fire, his eyes growing misty. "I owe Morty a debt of gratitude. I don't know what I would have done if I'd lost you to the likes of Chance LeRoy."

I laid my head on Mitch's shoulder. "You've got me now, for better or worse, Mr. Stone."

"Till death do us part, Mrs. Stone." He kissed the top of my head.

Morty suddenly appeared from out of nowhere, but this time Mitch didn't jump. Guess he was finally getting used to the other man in my life. I frowned when I saw he had that same rusted horseshoe in his mouth. He set it on the coffee table by our crossed feet, looked us both in the eye, and then disappeared.

I reached forward and picked up the horseshoe, once again feeling a strong energy, but not getting anything else from it.

"What do you think he's trying to tell us?" Mitch asked.

"I'm not sure, but I feel like it's connected to him somehow." I set the horseshoe back down. "I'll have to meditate on that one for a bit, but right now I have something else on my mind, Mr. Stone."

"And what would that be, Mrs. Stone?"

"Babies."

His Adam's apple bobbed once, and he stared at me for a moment.

"What's the matter?" I asked. "Cold feet?"

"Nope. They've never been warmer," he responded, then lowered his lips to mine.

ABOUT THE AUTHOR

Kari Lee Townsend is a National Bestselling Author of mysteries & a tween superhero series. She also writes romance and women's fiction as Kari Lee Harmon. With a background in English education, she's now a full-time writer, wife to her own superhero, mom of 3 sons, 1 darling diva, 1 daughter-in-law & 2 lovable fur babies. These days you'll find her walking her dogs or hard at work on her next story, living a blessed life.

OTHER BOOKS BY KARI LEE HARMON

Printed in the USA
CPSIA information can be obtained
at www.ICGtesting.com
LVHW03084530062 4
784301LV00034B/1325

9 781648 393594